BEES

COOL COMMUNICATORS

KATIE
LAJINESS

Big Buddy Books
An Imprint of Abdo Publishing
abdopublishing.com

AWESOME ANIMAL
POWERS

abdopublishing.com

Published by Abdo Publishing, a division of ABDO, PO Box 398166, Minneapolis, Minnesota 55439.
Copyright © 2019 by Abdo Consulting Group, Inc. International copyrights reserved in all countries.
No part of this book may be reproduced in any form without written permission from the publisher.
Big Buddy Books™ is a trademark and logo of Abdo Publishing.

Printed in the United States of America, North Mankato, Minnesota.
052018
092018

THIS BOOK CONTAINS
RECYCLED MATERIALS

Cover Photo: Antagain/Getty Images.
Interior Photos: © Harold Lloyd/Getty Images (p. 9); 5D2/Getty Images (p. 5); Antagain/Getty
    Images (pp. 7, 30); dimarik/Getty Images (p. 17); FrankRamspott/Getty Images (p. 11); Justin
    Sullivan/Getty Images News (p. 21); kozorog/Getty Images (p. 29); Matt Cardy/Getty Images
    News (p. 23); Philip Thompson / EyeEm/Getty Images (p. 27); Russ Henry / EyeEm/Getty Images
    (p. 19); Sean Gallup/Getty Images News (pp. 15, 25); Warrenrandalcarr/Getty Images (p. 7).

Coordinating Series Editor: Tamara L. Britton
Contributing Editor: Jill Roesler
Graphic Design: Jenny Christensen, Erika Weldon

Library of Congress Control Number: 2017961388

Publisher's Cataloging-in-Publication Data

Names: Lajiness, Katie, author.
Title: Bees: Cool communicators / by Katie Lajiness.
Other titles: Cool communicators
Description: Minneapolis, Minnesota : Abdo Publishing, 2019. | Series: Awesome animal
    powers | Includes online resources and index.
Identifiers: ISBN 9781532114977 (lib.bdg.) | ISBN 9781532155697 (ebook)
Subjects: LCSH: Bees--Juvenile literature. | Bees--Behavior--Juvenile literature. | Animal
    communication--Juvenile literature.
Classification: DDC 595.799--dc23

CONTENTS

THE BEE

The world is full of awesome, powerful animals. Bees live in almost every country of the world. They are cool **communicators**. They dance to show other bees where to collect pollen and nectar.

DID YOU KNOW?

Bees buzz by beating their wings 230 times a second!

The garden bumblebee has a tongue as long as its body. It uncurls its long tongue to get nectar deep inside plants.

BOLD BODIES

Like many insects, bees have six legs. On their legs are little baskets for collecting pollen.

Bees have two sets of wings. The front set is large and the rear set is smaller. And they have two big eyes and three small ones.

If a honeybee stings a human, the stinger will stay in the human's skin. A honeybee will die without its stinger. But a bumblebee can use its stinger many times.

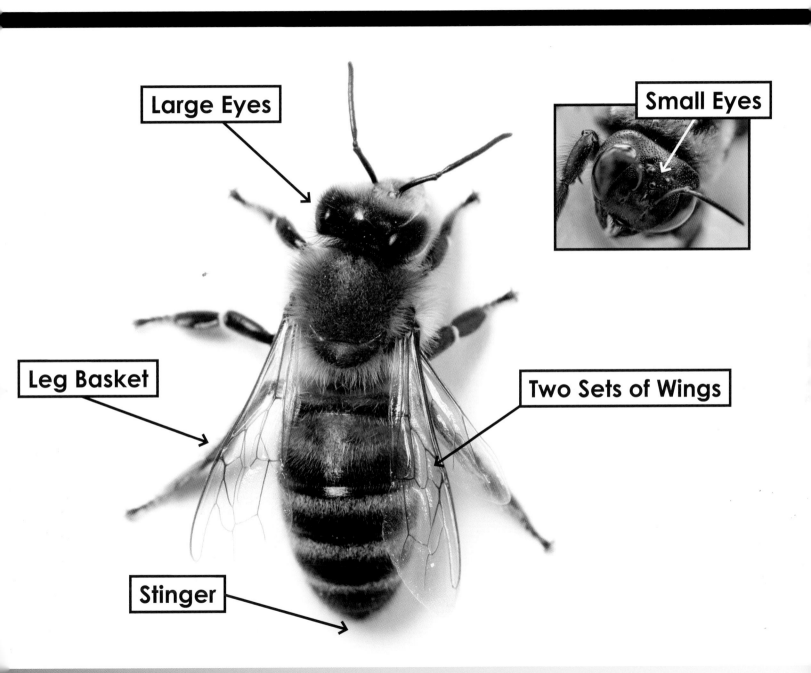

Large Eyes

Small Eyes

Leg Basket

Two Sets of Wings

Stinger

THAT'S AWESOME!

Worker bees **communicate** with other bees by dancing. They do a special dance to tell others where to find nectar, pollen, or water. The way a bee dances tells other bees how far away the food is.

DID YOU KNOW?

Most bees are hairy. Flower pollen sticks to the hairs for easy collection.

Bees pause between dances to offer other bees a taste of the nectar. The sample tells other bees what type of flower it is from.

The two common types of dances are the round dance and the waggle dance. When the bee **performs** the round dance it means food is close by.

The waggle dance is an 8 shape with a waggle in the middle. It tells other bees how to find nectar that is farther from the hive.

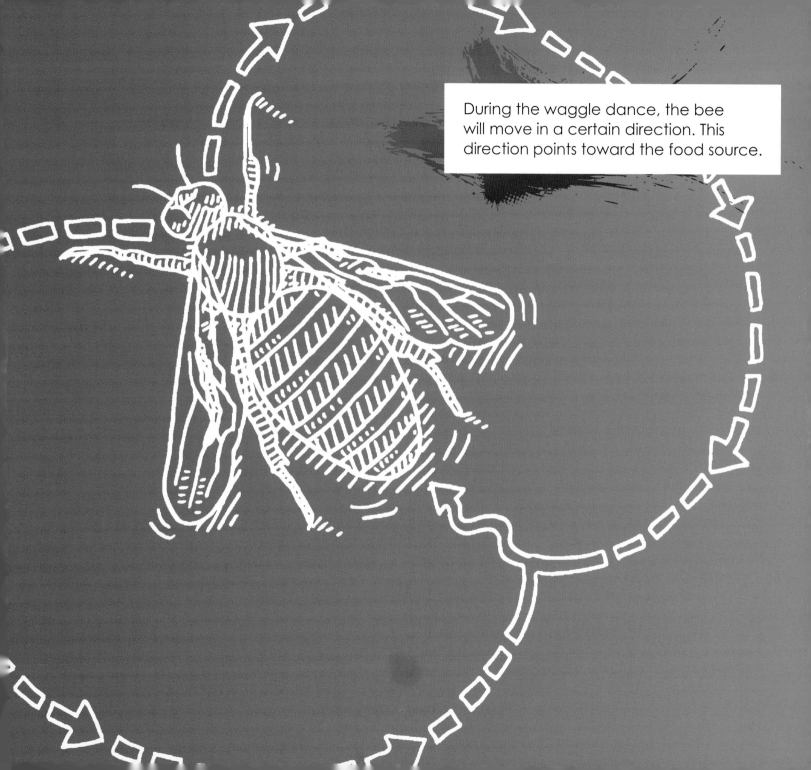

During the waggle dance, the bee will move in a certain direction. This direction points toward the food source.

WHERE IN THE

Social bees live together in a hive. Hives are found in trees or between rocks. Other bees live alone. They rest on plant stems or between flower petals.

Around the world, bees live wherever there are flowers. Bees can live in grasslands, forests, swamps, and gardens.

WORLD?

ARCTIC OCEAN

North America

Europe

Asia

PACIFIC OCEAN

NORTH ATLANTIC OCEAN

Africa

PACIFIC OCEAN

South America

INDIAN OCEAN

Australia

SOUTH ATLANTIC OCEAN

N
W   E
S

DAILY LIFE

Bees are often found buzzing near flowers. In one trip, a bee can visit 50 different flowers looking for nectar and pollen. Then it uses its long tongue to drink nectar. Some types of bees use nectar to make honey.

DID YOU KNOW?

Humans began collecting honey more than 9,000 years ago!

Honey is the only food made by insects that humans can eat.

Honeybees spend most of their time making honey. Once the worker bees return to the hive, they pass the nectar to other bees. They pass it until all water within it disappears. Now it is honey. Bees store honey on a grid called a **honeycomb**.

Only female bees have stingers. They use their stingers to protect against attackers.

A BEE'S LIFE

Bees are busy all day. Every honeybee in the **colony** has a job. There is only one queen bee. She is the largest bee. And, she lays all the eggs. She can lay up to 1,500 eggs a day!

Bees stay active during the day.
At night, they stay in their hives.

Drone bees are male. They **mate** with the queen to make eggs. Worker bees are female. They feed the queen, build the hive, and make honey. Some collect pollen and nectar.

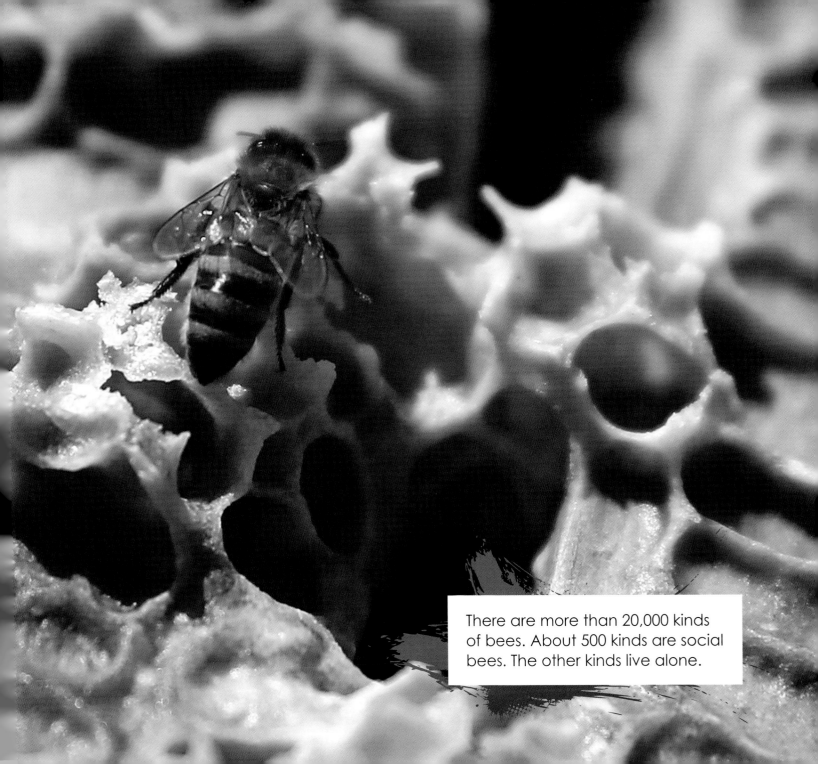

There are more than 20,000 kinds of bees. About 500 kinds are social bees. The other kinds live alone.

FAVORITE FOODS

Bees take pollen and nectar from many types of flowers. Pollen has everything honeybees need to stay healthy. The nectar is later turned into honey.

Young honeybees also eat honey. But those chosen to become future queens eat royal jelly. This white liquid helps queens become twice the size of other bees.

Children under 12 months old should not eat honey. This food contains bacteria that can make a baby very sick.

BIRTH

After a male and a queen bee **mate**, she lays eggs inside a wax cell. Each egg goes through many growth stages. These stages take about three weeks. When the bees are ready, they chew their way out of the cells.

Queens are fully grown after about 16 days. Worker bees need about 21 days to grow. And drone bees take about 24 days.

DEVELOPMENT

A bee's life span varies. After about three weeks, the bee becomes an adult. Worker bees born during the spring or summer may only live about seven weeks. However, queen honeybees can live up to five years.

Worker bees care for the eggs. Some workers will check on the eggs up to 1,000 times a day!

FUTURE

The earth needs bees. About one-third of the world's food grows because bees **pollinate** the plants. But there are many things that can harm bees. Their **habitat** is disappearing because of a loss of **natural resources**.

Luckily, many people work hard to save the bees. Even planting a flower garden can help the bees live.

As the earth continues to warm, flowers may grow in new areas. If the plants are too far away, the bees may not be able to reach them.

FAST FACTS

ANIMAL TYPE: Insect

SIZE: Between 0.5 and 1.5 inches (13 to 38 mm)

WEIGHT: 0.001 to 0.03 ounces (0.04 to 0.85 g)

HABITAT: Near blooming trees, plants, and flowers

DIET: Pollen, honey, and royal jelly

AWESOME ANIMAL POWER:
Bees perform special dances to communicate with each other.

GLOSSARY

colony a group of animals of one kind living together.

communicate (kuh-MYOO-nuh-kayt) to share knowledge, thoughts, or feelings. A communicator is one that communicates something.

habitat a place where a living thing is naturally found.

honeycomb a mass of wax cells built by honeybees in their nest to contain young bees and stores of honey.

mate to join as a couple in order to reproduce, or have babies.

natural resource useful and valued supplies from nature.

perform to carry out an action or pattern of behavior.

pollinate to transfer from one flower or plant to another. This helps the plant grow fruit and seeds.

ONLINE RESOURCES

Booklinks
NONFICTION NETWORK
FREE! ONLINE NONFICTION RESOURCES

To learn more about bees, visit **abdobooklinks.com**. These links are routinely monitored and updated to provide the most current information available.

INDEX